On the fresh snow,
as in my heart,
footprints, traces.

Fox's Garden

Princesse Camcam

ENCHANTED LION BOOKS
NEW YORK

Titles in our Stories Without Words series:
The Chicken Thief by Béatrice Rodriguez
Fox and Hen Together by Béatrice Rodriguez
Rooster's Revenge by Béatrice Rodriguez
Ice by Arthur Geisert
The Giant Seed by Arthur Geisert
Bear Despair by Gaëtan Dorémus
Coyote Run by Gaëtan Dorémus

www.enchantedlionbooks.com

First American edition published in 2014 by
Enchanted Lion Books, 351 Van Brunt Street, Brooklyn, NY 11231
Translation © 2014 by Enchanted Lion Books
Originally published in France by Éditions Autrement © 2013 as Une rencontre
All rights reserved under International and Pan-American Copyright Conventions
Library of Congress Control Number: 2014934817
ISBN: 978-1-59270-167-4
Printed in April 2014 in China by South China Printing Company